Published by Scholastic Inc., 90 Old Sherman Turnpike,
Danbury, Connecticut 06816.

For information regarding permission, write to:
Disney Licensed Publishing, 114 Fifth Avenue,
New York, New York 10011.

ISBN 0-7172-7831-X

Printed in the U.S.A.
First printing, March 2005

Disney · PIXAR

FINDING NEMO

SCHOLASTIC INC.

New York   Toronto   London   Auckland   Sydney
Mexico City   New Delhi   Hong Kong   Buenos Aires

"**C**'mon, Dad!" Nemo
called out. "It's time for school!"
The little clownfish Nemo was
ready for his first day of school. One
of Nemo's fins was smaller than the
other, so he was not a great swimmer.
Nemo, however, didn't let it slow him down.
But his father, Marlin, wasn't ready for
Nemo to go. He was very protective of his
son, and he worried—a lot.

"All right," Marlin reluctantly agreed. Then he went over the safety rules.

"So . . . first we check to see that the coast is clear," coached Marlin as he swam out of their anemone home. "We go out . . . and back in. And then we go out . . . and back in. And then—"

"Dad . . . ," Nemo interrupted. He tugged on his father's fin and pulled him out at last.

Soon Nemo and Marlin
arrived at the school yard.
The teacher Mr. Ray sailed in to
take the children on a field trip.
"Bye, Dad!" Nemo shouted as
Mr. Ray swam away.
        "Bye, Son!" Marlin called.
        "Be safe."

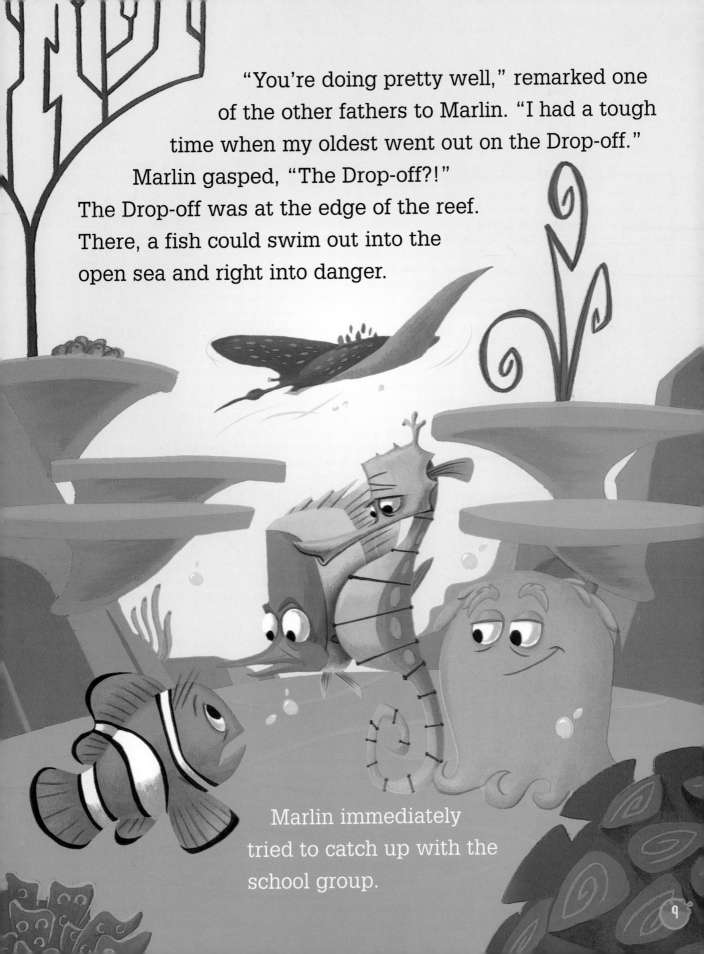

"You're doing pretty well," remarked one of the other fathers to Marlin. "I had a tough time when my oldest went out on the Drop-off." Marlin gasped, "The Drop-off?!" The Drop-off was at the edge of the reef. There, a fish could swim out into the open sea and right into danger.

Marlin immediately tried to catch up with the school group.

Meanwhile, Nemo and his new friends Tad, Sheldon, and Pearl sneaked away to look out over the edge of the Drop-off.

"I know what that is—a butt!" said Tad, pointing up at the bottom of a boat. Then Sheldon dared them to see who could swim closest to it.

Finally, it was Nemo's turn. "Come on, Nemo! How far can you go?" Tad challenged.

"Oh, um . . . my dad says it's not safe," Nemo said, not moving.

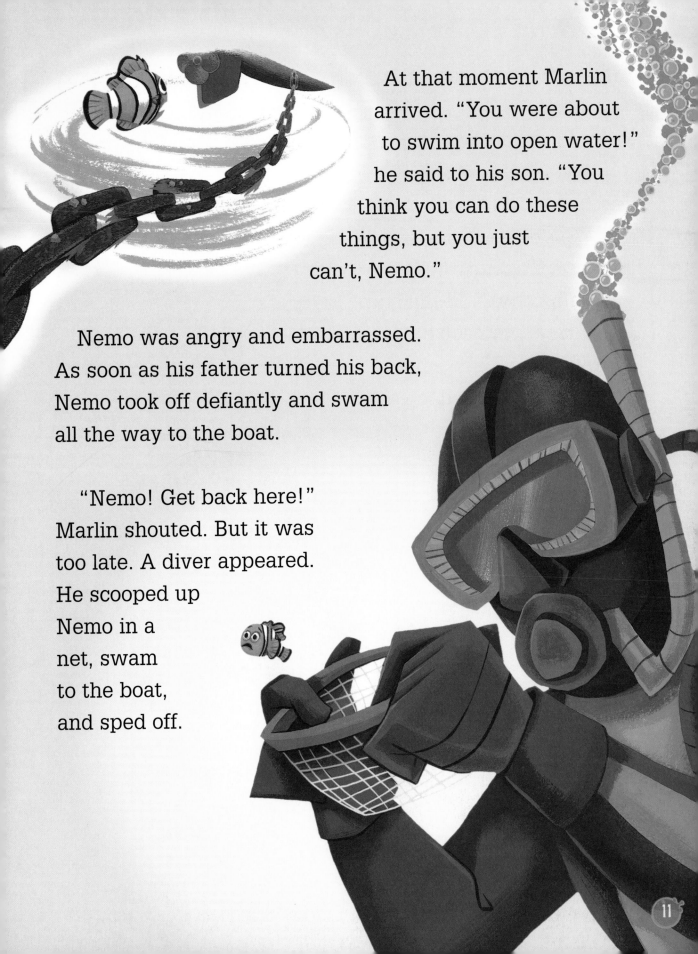

At that moment Marlin arrived. "You were about to swim into open water!" he said to his son. "You think you can do these things, but you just can't, Nemo."

Nemo was angry and embarrassed. As soon as his father turned his back, Nemo took off defiantly and swam all the way to the boat.

"Nemo! Get back here!" Marlin shouted. But it was too late. A diver appeared. He scooped up Nemo in a net, swam to the boat, and sped off.

Marlin couldn't swim
fast enough to catch up
with the boat. When he swam
into a stream of fish to ask for
help, he slammed into one of them.

"Sir? Are you okay?" asked a friendly blue fish.
"Hi, I'm Dory."

"I have to find the boat!" said Marlin.

"Hey, I've seen a boat.
Follow me!" she said.

Marlin followed Dory until she suddenly turned
around and said, "Stop following me!"

Marlin was confused until Dory explained, "I suffer
from short-term memory loss."

Marlin turned to leave
and found himself facing
a shark! Bruce the shark
invited them to a "party"
in a sunken submarine.
The "party" was a
meeting of sharks
who were trying
not to eat fish.

While there, Marlin
spotted a diver's mask
that had been dropped
by Nemo's captor. Marlin
hoped the writing on
the mask could help him
find his son.

"Ugh! What do these markings mean! I can't read
human!" exclaimed Marlin.

"Well, we gotta find a fish that can!" encouraged Dory.
They both grabbed the mask, which snapped and hit Dory
in the face.

"Ow!" Dory cried as blood trickled from her nose.

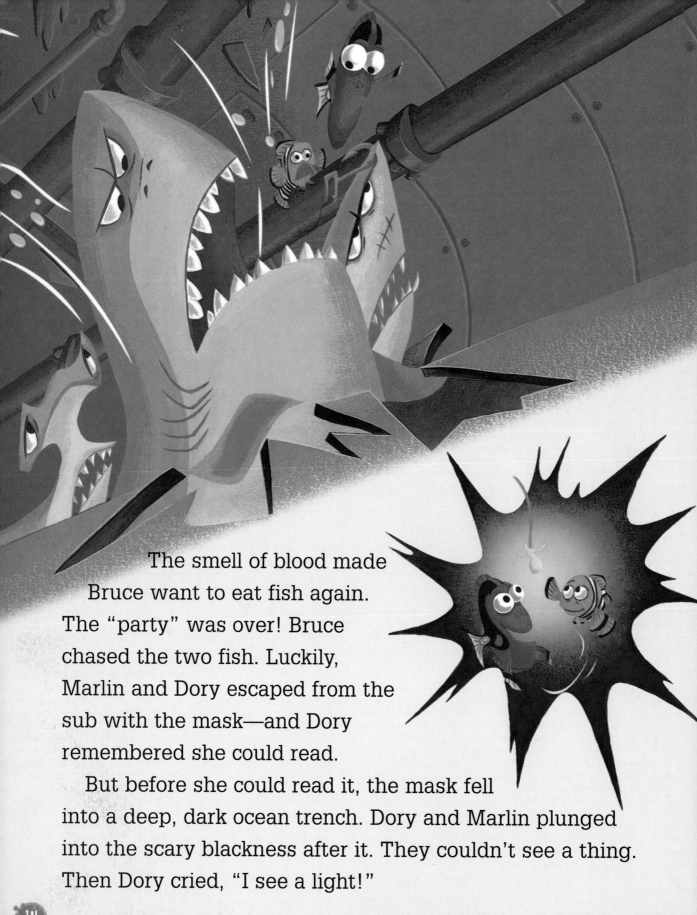

The smell of blood made
Bruce want to eat fish again.
The "party" was over! Bruce
chased the two fish. Luckily,
Marlin and Dory escaped from the
sub with the mask—and Dory
remembered she could read.

But before she could read it, the mask fell
into a deep, dark ocean trench. Dory and Marlin plunged
into the scary blackness after it. They couldn't see a thing.
Then Dory cried, "I see a light!"

But the light turned out to be an anglerfish.

As the anglerfish chased them, its light fell on something. "Hey, look! A mask," Dory shouted.

"Read it!" Marlin ordered, trying to keep the anglerfish away from Dory.

"Bring him closer. I need the light," Dory answered.

Marlin led the anglerfish back and forth while Dory read the address on the mask. Then Dory and Marlin escaped in the nick of time!

"P. Sherman, 42 Wallaby Way, Sydney," said Dory proudly, as they swam off.

"Now where is that?" wondered Marlin.

It turned out that 42 Wallaby Way was a dentist's
office in Sydney, Australia. The diver who had caught
Nemo was the dentist, and he put the little fish into
his office aquarium. The aquarium was home to an
interesting group of fish known as the Tank Gang.

A friendly pelican named Nigel was perched
on the dentist's windowsill visiting the Tank Gang.
From them, Nemo found out that he was going to
become a gift for the dentist's niece, Darla.

The Tank Gang told Nemo that the dentist had given
Darla a fish last year, and it hadn't survived.

"I have to get back to my dad!" cried Nemo, horrified.

The leader of the Tank Gang, Gill, reassured Nemo
that they would find a way to escape
before Darla arrived.

Meanwhile back in the ocean . . . .

"P. Sherman, 42 Wallaby Way, Sydney!" Dory proudly repeated the address over and over.

Marlin asked a school of moonfish if they could tell him how to get to Sydney. The moonfish didn't want to help Marlin, but they were happy to help Dory. They formed themselves into an arrow pointing in the direction of Sydney.

"Great!" said Marlin,
rushing off in the direction they had indicated.

"Oh, hey, ma'am?" the moonfish said to Dory. "When you come to the trench, swim through it—not over it."

"I'll remember!" said Dory, as she hurried to catch up with Marlin.

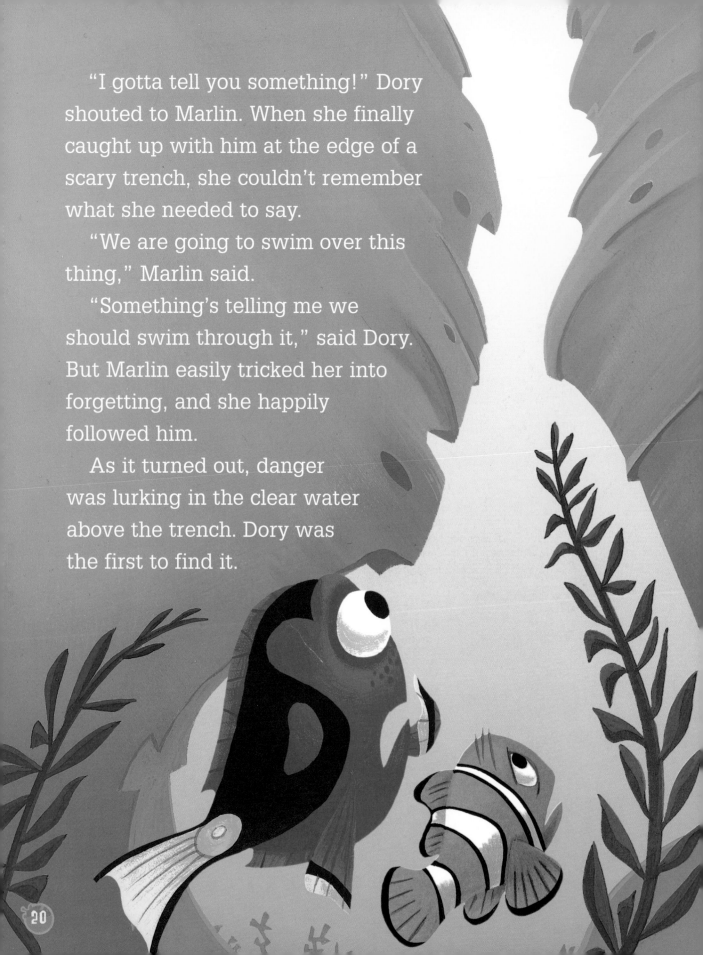

"I gotta tell you something!" Dory shouted to Marlin. When she finally caught up with him at the edge of a scary trench, she couldn't remember what she needed to say.

"We are going to swim over this thing," Marlin said.

"Something's telling me we should swim through it," said Dory. But Marlin easily tricked her into forgetting, and she happily followed him.

As it turned out, danger was lurking in the clear water above the trench. Dory was the first to find it.

"Ow!" Dory yelled. A baby jellyfish had stung her. Marlin rushed over and shooed the baby away.

"Let's be thankful this time it was just a little one," Marlin said. But then the two fish realized that they were surrounded by hundreds of jellyfish.

"This is bad," said Marlin.

But Dory was giggling. "Hey! Watch this!" she said, bouncing on the tops of the jellyfish. Marlin quickly made up a game of jumping on the jellyfish tops. But there was one rule: "You can't touch the tentacles," Marlin explained. The race began. Marlin quickly hopped out of the jellyfish forest. But when he turned around, Dory was nowhere in sight. "DORY!" Marlin cried. Then he saw her caught in a jellyfish's tentacles. Marlin swam back to his friend and dragged her out of the jellyfish forest. Then everything went black.

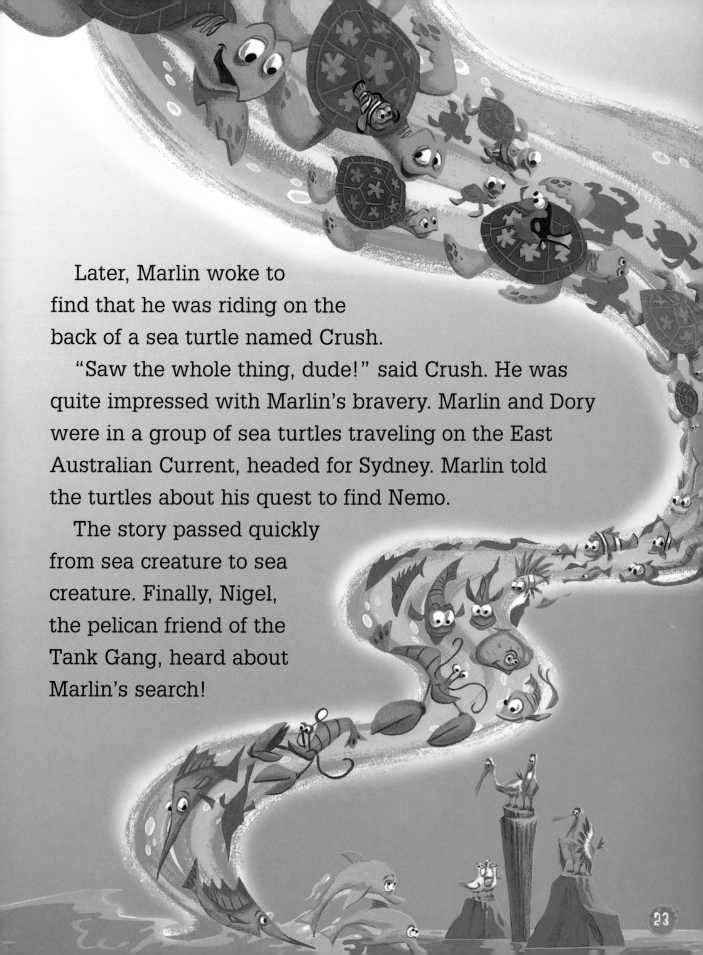

Later, Marlin woke to
find that he was riding on the
back of a sea turtle named Crush.

"Saw the whole thing, dude!" said Crush. He was
quite impressed with Marlin's bravery. Marlin and Dory
were in a group of sea turtles traveling on the East
Australian Current, headed for Sydney. Marlin told
the turtles about his quest to find Nemo.

The story passed quickly
from sea creature to sea
creature. Finally, Nigel,
the pelican friend of the
Tank Gang, heard about
Marlin's search!

The ride on the current was great fun for
Marlin and Dory, but suddenly Crush called out,
"Get ready! Your exit's comin' up, man!"

"Thank you, dude-Crush!" Marlin shouted as
he and Dory left the current.

They soon found themselves in very murky water,
looking for Sydney.

"Let's ask somebody for directions," suggested
Dory, spotting what looked like a small fish far away.
"There's somebody!"

"It's a fish we don't know. It could ingest us!" Marlin said nervously.

But Dory continued. "Woo-hoo! Little fellah?!" she called. But soon Marlin and Dory discovered that the "little fish" was a giant whale! In one big mouthful, it swallowed them both.

"We're in a whale!" shouted Marlin.

"Wow! A whale? You know, I speak whale." Dory listened carefully to the whale's loud moans. "He said we should go to the back of the throat."

Marlin was irritated. "Of course he wants us to go there. That's . . . eating us!"

"He says it's time to let go," Dory told Marlin.

So Marlin let go. Suddenly he and Dory soon found themselves being shot out of the whale's spout. They flew into air, then splashed back into the sea.

When the two of them had recovered, they realized they were in Sydney Harbor.

"You were right, Dory. We made it! We're going to find my son!" cheered Marlin. "All we have to do is find the boat that took him."

But Sydney Harbor was full
of boats. The two fish searched
all through the night.

The next morning, a hungry
pelican scooped the exhausted
pair of fish into his beak, as he
flew back towards land.

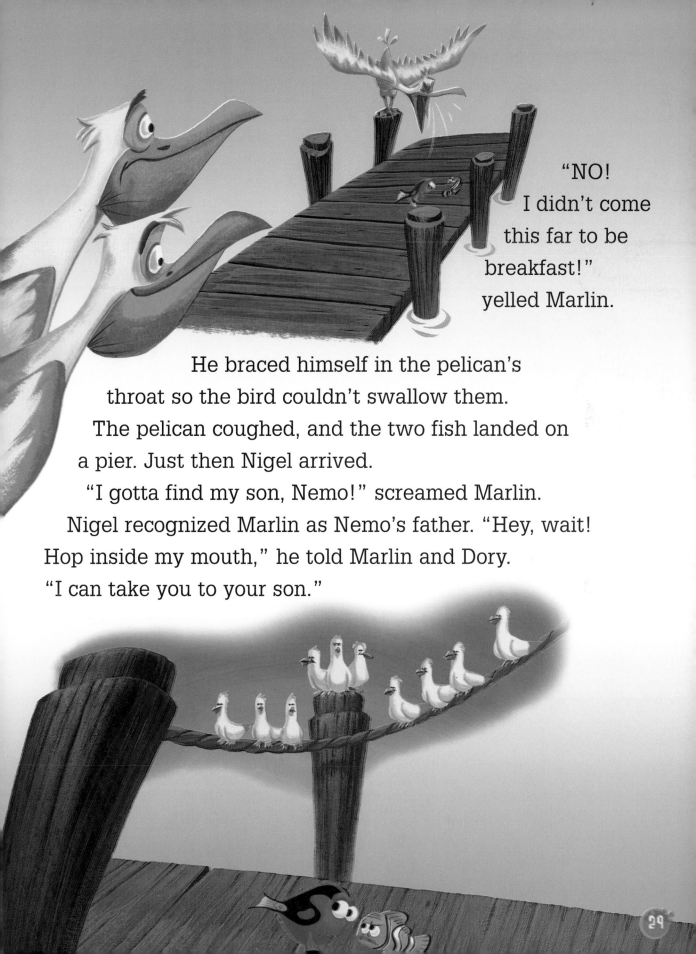

"NO!
I didn't come
this far to be
breakfast!"
yelled Marlin.

He braced himself in the pelican's
throat so the bird couldn't swallow them.
The pelican coughed, and the two fish landed on
a pier. Just then Nigel arrived.

"I gotta find my son, Nemo!" screamed Marlin.

Nigel recognized Marlin as Nemo's father. "Hey, wait!
Hop inside my mouth," he told Marlin and Dory.
"I can take you to your son."

Back at the dentist's office, things were going badly for little Nemo. Niece Darla was due to arrive any moment! The dentist had Nemo in a water-filled plastic bag, ready to give to her.

The dentist placed the bag with the panicked Nemo on a table.

The Tank Gang instructed Nemo to push the side of the bag so it would roll out of the open window. But just as Nemo succeeded in getting the bag rolling, the dentist noticed.

"Oh, that would be a nasty fall," the dentist said, catching the bag and setting it down on a tray. Suddenly the door to the office slammed open . . . and Darla stomped in!

But Nemo had an idea. He pretended to be dead, hoping that the dentist would flush him down the toilet. From there, Nemo planned to swim to the ocean.

"Hello, Darla, honey!" said the dentist to his niece.

"Oh no," he murmured when he noticed the motionless Nemo. The dentist quickly hid the bag behind his back, so Darla wouldn't see it.

Moments later the window burst open.
In flew Nigel, carrying Dory and Marlin.

"What the—?" exclaimed the dentist
when Nigel collided with him. The dentist
dropped the bag holding Nemo onto a tray.
A sharp instrument on the tray tore a small
hole in the bag.

From his view in Nigel's beak, Marlin spotted
Nemo and thought his son was dead. "Nemo!"
he cried.

Nemo heard his father's voice, but
it was too late. The dentist had
closed Nigel's beak and shoved
him out the window.

In the confusion, Darla had picked up the bag and swung it back and forth chanting, "Fishy! Fishy!"

Nemo poured out of the hole in the bag and became stranded on a dental tool.

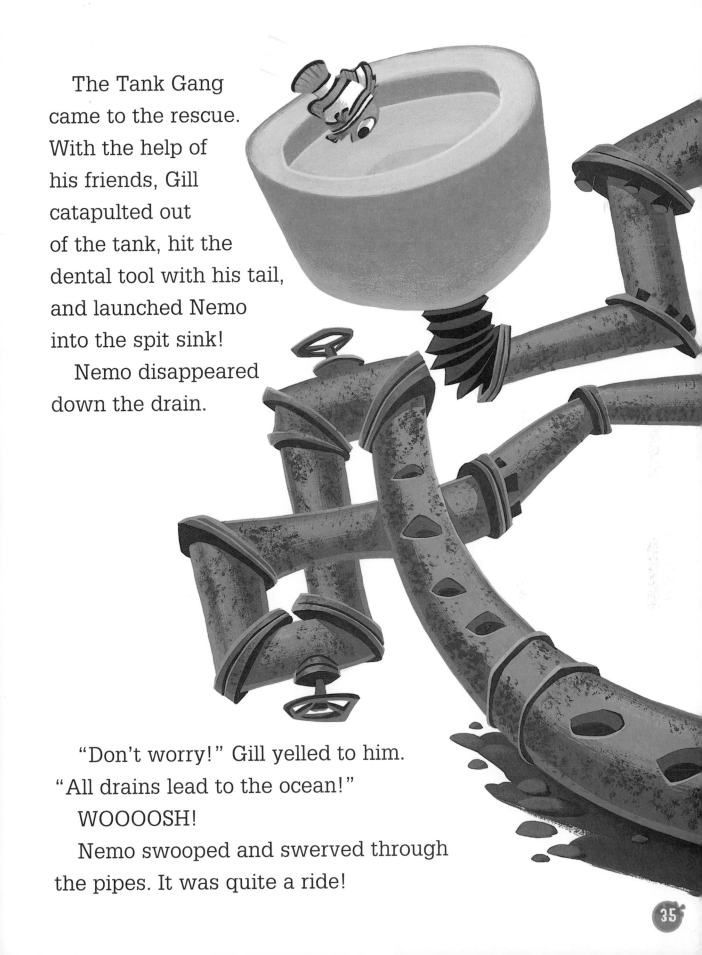

The Tank Gang came to the rescue. With the help of his friends, Gill catapulted out of the tank, hit the dental tool with his tail, and launched Nemo into the spit sink!

Nemo disappeared down the drain.

"Don't worry!" Gill yelled to him. "All drains lead to the ocean!"

WOOOOSH!

Nemo swooped and swerved through the pipes. It was quite a ride!

35

Back in Sydney Harbor, Marlin sadly said good-bye
to Nigel and Dory. He swam past two crabs on a
drainage pipe, and then he joined a school
of grouper fish. Marlin started the
long swim home.

Nemo, meanwhile, ended his ride through the pipes of Sydney. He popped up through a hole next to the very same two crabs.

"Oy! Gotta live one here!" said one crab.

"Have you seen my dad?" Nemo asked. But he soon realized that the crabs were only interested in catching and eating him. So off Nemo swam—in the opposite direction that his father had gone.

Before long, Nemo found Dory swimming in circles and crying.

"I don't know where I am . . . I think I lost somebody, but I . . . need to remember . . . ."

"I'm Nemo," said the little fish. "I'm looking for someone, too."

"Nemo. That's a nice name," murmured Dory, not paying much attention. The two fish searched together for a while.

Suddenly Dory remembered! "NEMO!" She grabbed the little guy's face tight with her fins. "You're not dead! And your father . . . ."

"You know my father?" asked Nemo.
But Dory was already moving.
"This way! Quick!"

Dory and
Nemo swam over
to the two crabs on the
pipe and asked them whether
they had seen Marlin.

"I'm not tellin'. And there's no way you're
gonna make me," one of the crabs replied.

Dory grabbed the crab and thrust him above
the water. The crab quickly gave Dory and Nemo
the directions they needed.

Nemo and Dory rushed to the fishing grounds
to look for Marlin.

"Dad! Dad!" yelled Nemo, when he finally
spotted Marlin in a crowd of grouper fish.

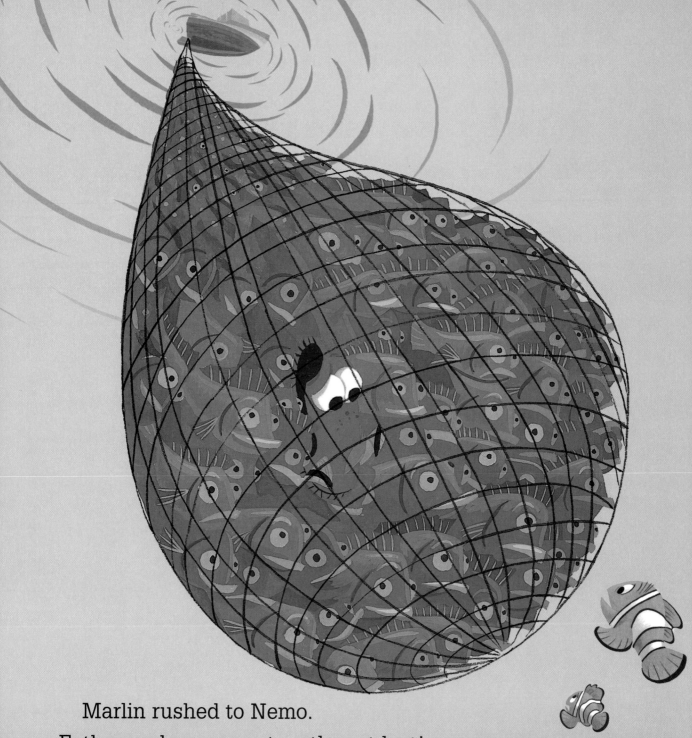

Marlin rushed to Nemo.

Father and son were together at last!

"Look out!" yelled Dory as an enormous fishing net suddenly swept past them. The net missed Nemo and Marlin, but Dory and the grouper fish were caught.

"HEELLPP!!!" screamed Dory.

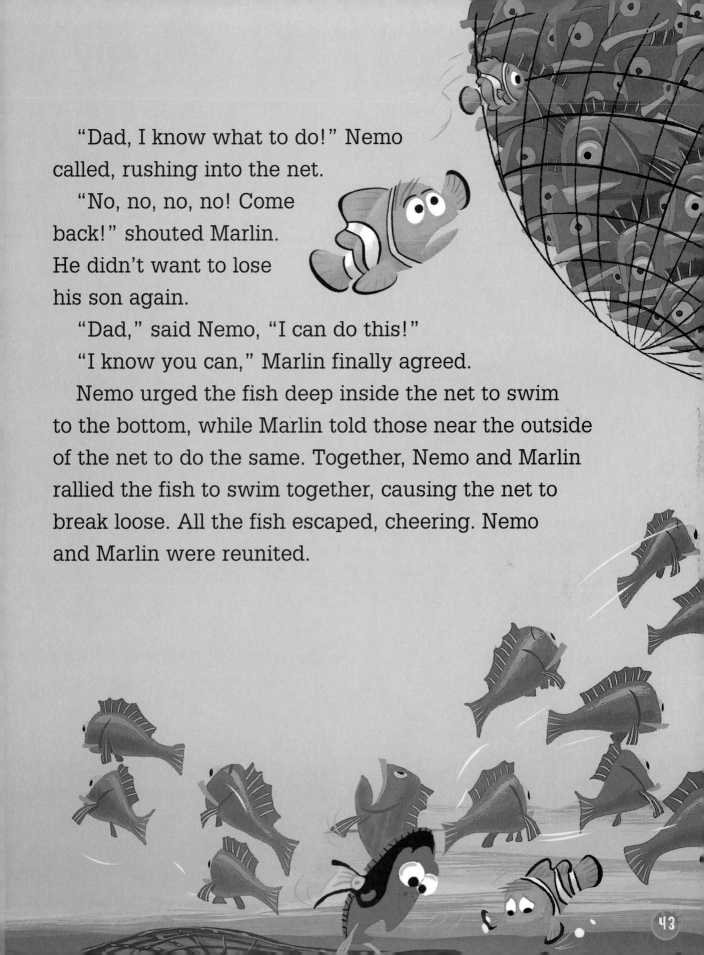

"Dad, I know what to do!" Nemo called, rushing into the net.

"No, no, no, no! Come back!" shouted Marlin. He didn't want to lose his son again.

"Dad," said Nemo, "I can do this!"

"I know you can," Marlin finally agreed.

Nemo urged the fish deep inside the net to swim to the bottom, while Marlin told those near the outside of the net to do the same. Together, Nemo and Marlin rallied the fish to swim together, causing the net to break loose. All the fish escaped, cheering. Nemo and Marlin were reunited.

Nemo and Marlin brought Dory back
to their reef. Nemo started school
again. He was overjoyed to be with his
friends and Mr. Ray, the schoolteacher.

Just as Mr. Ray started to pull away, Nemo looked back at his dad. Then Nemo asked Mr. Ray to wait. Nemo raced back and gave his dad a big hug. "Love ya, Dad," said Nemo.

"I love you, too, Son," said Marlin, holding tightly. "Now go have an adventure."

THE END

EYE SPY

Make a splash! Dive back into the story to catch these pictures.